Thanksgiving
Turkey Trouble

by ABBY KLEIN

illustrated by
JOHN MCKINLEY

THE BLUE SKY PRESS
An Imprint of Scholastic Inc. • New York

To my family:
I am thankful for you everyday . . .
I love you!
love,
A. K.

THE BLUE SKY PRESS

Text copyright © 2008 by Abby Klein
Illustrations copyright © 2008 by John McKinley
All rights reserved.

Special thanks to Robert Martin Staenberg.

No part of this publication may be reproduced, stored in
a retrieval system, or transmitted in any form or by any means,
electronic, mechanical, photocopying, recording, or otherwise,
without written permission of the publisher. For information
regarding permission, please write to: Permissions Department,
Scholastic Inc., 557 Broadway, New York, New York 10012.
SCHOLASTIC, THE BLUE SKY PRESS, and associated logos are
trademarks and/or registered trademarks of Scholastic Inc.
Library of Congress catalog card number: 2008002933
ISBN-13: 978-0-439-89595-8 / ISBN-10: 0-439-89595-2
10 9 8 7 6 5 4 3   08 09 10 11 12 13
Printed in the United States of America 40
First printing, September 2008

CHAPTERS

I have a problem.

A really, really, big problem.

My class is doing a play

for Thanksgiving, and

I'm afraid I'll get

the worst part!

Let me tell you about it.

CHAPTER 1

Let's Give Thanks

"Listen, everyone," said our teacher, Mrs. Wushy. "Thanksgiving is coming up, so I'd like us all to take a minute and think about the things we are thankful for. I'm going to make a list of your suggestions."

Chloe's hand shot up. "Oh, I know lots of things I'm thankful for."

"That's wonderful, Chloe. Why don't you tell us about one thing."

"This should be good," I whispered to my best friend, Robbie.

"Yeah," Robbie whispered back. "I bet she's probably going to say she's thankful for red nail polish."

"Chloe, we're waiting," said Mrs. Wushy.

"I'm thinking. I'm thinking," said Chloe, wrinkling up her nose. "It's just so hard to choose only one thing."

Max let out a huge sigh. "Hey, Little Miss Priss, we haven't got all day."

Chloe turned and glared at Max. "It's not

your turn. It's mine, and I was about to say, 'I am thankful for my really beautiful, expensive dresses' when you interrupted me."

My other good friend, Jessie, leaned over to me. "Is she serious?"

"Oh, she's serious all right."

Mrs. Wushy stared at Chloe for a moment and then said, "Yes, well, that's nice, but I was hoping we could think of things that are a bit more personal."

"Oh, you mean like jewelry?"

Robbie shook his head. "Is she for real?"

"No, Chloe, more like things you can't buy in a store."

"I don't get it," said Chloe.

"Of course you don't," Jessie muttered under her breath. "I think I might have an idea, Mrs. Wushy."

"Great, Jessie. What is it?"

"Family. I am thankful for my family."

"Excellent. That is exactly the kind of thing I was looking for."

"I feel so lucky to have my mom and my *abuela*, my grandma, living with me."

Mrs. Wushy wrote the word "family" at the top of the list.

"I have one," Robbie said, raising his hand. "A home, a place to live. Every time I see a homeless person on the street, I think about how lucky I am that I have a place to sleep at night."

"Another excellent idea," said Mrs. Wushy, adding the word "home." "I'd like each person in the class to add something to our list. Who'd like to go next?"

"Food!" yelled Max. As usual, he didn't raise his hand. He just blurted out the answer.

"Thank you, Max. Food is a good suggestion, but you need to remember to raise your hand and not call out."

"Hey, that's not fair," Chloe whined. "You said you didn't want things you can buy in a store. You can buy food in a store."

"That's true, Chloe," said Mrs. Wushy, "but food is something we can't live without."

"Well, I can't live without my expensive dresses, so why can't they go on the list?"

Mrs. Wushy let out a big sigh and then called on the next person.

Kids made all kinds of suggestions for the list: nature, friends, pets, and grandparents.

My turn was next, and I couldn't think

of anything else to say. All of my ideas were already on the list.

"Freddy, how about you?" said Mrs. Wushy. "You haven't given us a word for the list yet."

"Ummmm, ummmmm."

"Freddy, you've had a lot of time to think. We're running out of time."

"Love." The word just slipped out of my mouth before I could stop it. I could hear all the kids snickering.

Then Max started singing, "Freddy and Jessie sitting in a tree. K-I-S-S-I-N-G. First comes love . . ."

"Max, that is enough!" said Mrs. Wushy, and she pointed to a chair. "Go sit in that chair. You are in time-out." Then she turned back to me. "I am sorry about that, Freddy. I think what you said is beautiful. I think we are all thankful for love. I don't even want to think about what the world would be like without love."

"Nice one," Robbie whispered.

"Thanks."

"Mrs. Wushy sure liked it. That'll probably put you on her good list."

"OK, boys and girls. You all did a great job thinking of things you are thankful for. Now I have a special surprise for you."

"Oooh, I just love surprises," Chloe squealed, clapping her hands together. "Is it a present? Is there one for everybody?"

"No, Chloe, it's not a present," Mrs. Wushy answered. You could tell she was starting to get irritated.

"Oh," said Chloe, disappointed.

"We are going to do a little play for your parents about the story of Thanksgiving, and we'll also include some of these things we are thankful for."

"Yeah! A play! A play!" everyone cheered.

"I love plays," said Jessie.

"I do, too. Suzie told me this play is really fun. She got to do it when she was in Mrs. Wushy's class."

"Cool."

"Boys and girls, you will all get your parts tomorrow."

Everyone started yelling, "I want to be a Pilgrim! I want to be an Indian!"

"Quiet down, everybody. I know you are all excited, but you will have to wait until tomorrow."

"Awwwhhhhhhh."

"And you do not get to choose your part. I will write down all the parts on little slips of paper, and you will pick one out of a hat. There will be no complaining. You get what you get, and you don't get upset."

"I hope I get a good part," said Jessie.

"Me, too," I said. "Me, too!"

CHAPTER 2

Pass the Potatoes, Please

That night at dinner my mom said, "I have some great news! Papa Dave and Grammy Rose are coming for Thanksgiving."

"Woo hoo!" I yelled, jumping up and down and pumping my fist in the air.

"I'm glad you're excited, Freddy. But please sit back down in your chair. You almost knocked the bowl of mashed potatoes on the floor."

"Sorry, Mom. I love when they come.

Grammy is the best cook. Is she going to make the turkey and stuffing?"

"Of course! What would Thanksgiving be without Grammy Rose's stuffing?"

"It *is* the best," my dad agreed.

"They called today to tell me they were going to be coming."

I jumped out of my chair again and sang, "They're coming! They're coming!" as I danced around the table.

"You're crazy," Suzie said. She made the cuckoo sign with her finger.

As I was dancing, I accidentally knocked into the table with my hip. The bowl of mashed potatoes went sailing off the table and landed in my dad's lap. I froze.

"Oh my goodness! Daniel, are you all right?" my mom asked, jumping out of her chair and running over to my dad. "Don't move. Let me get something to clean it up." She ran to the sink to get a sponge and some paper towels.

My dad looked furious. "Freddy! I know it

was an accident, but your mother already asked you once to stop fooling around at the table. Look what happened because you didn't listen to her. You need to be a better listener."

"Sorry, Dad."

My mom came over with the sponge and wiped the potato off my dad's pants.

"Now, Freddy, sit down, and I don't want you to get up again until we are finished with dinner. Do you understand?"

I quickly sat back down and stared at the floor. "Yes, Dad."

"Why don't we talk about something else?" said my mom. "Did anything exciting happen at school today?"

"I got one hundred percent on my spelling test," Suzie said, grinning from ear to ear.

"That's wonderful, honey. I am very proud of you."

"Whoop-de-doo," I muttered under my breath.

"Freddy, that is not very polite. You should be happy for your sister."

"Yeah, brat, you should be happy for me."

"I am not a brat."

"Yes you are."

"No I'm not!"

"Oh yes you are!"

"All right, you two. Enough!" my dad interrupted. "I'd like to eat my dinner in peace. Do you think maybe we could get through one dinner without the two of you fighting?"

We both stared at him.

"Well?"

"Yes," I mumbled.

"Suzie, how about you?"

"Yes."

"Great. Being nice to each other starts right . . . now."

"So, Freddy, what about you? Do you have any news from school?" my mom asked.

"Well, ummm, oh yeah! I just remembered.

Today Mrs. Wushy told us that we are going to do a Thanksgiving play for our parents."

"Remember at the beginning of the year I told you that you would get to do that in Mrs. Wushy's class?" Suzie said excitedly.

"I know. I've been waiting."

"It is so much fun! You get to wear costumes and paint the scenery."

"What part did you get?"

"I was a Pilgrim girl on the *Mayflower*."

"You looked so cute," my mom said. "I have pictures of you in the photo album wearing that adorable costume."

"I hope I get a good part."

"Of course you'll get a good part. There is no such thing as a bad part," said my mom.

"Well, actually, there is," Suzie said.

"What do you mean?"

"Somebody in the class has to be the Thanksgiving turkey."

"The turkey! No way! There is no way I'm going to dress up in some turkey costume in front of all my friends and their parents!"

"And don't forget Papa and Grammy."

"I'd be so embarrassed. I don't want Papa and Grammy to see me like that!"

"Well, when I was in Mrs. Wushy's class, you didn't get to choose your part."

"That's exactly what she told us today. She said that we're going to pick the parts out of a hat."

"Did she also say, 'You get what you get, and you don't get upset'?"

"Yeah," I muttered. "It's her favorite thing to say!"

"That sounds fair," my mom said. "Maybe you'll be a Pilgrim like your sister."

"I really want to be one of the Indians," I said as I got up out of my chair and started whooping and dancing around the table. "Look at me. I'm doing an Indian dance that Mrs. Wushy taught us today."

"Freddy!" my mom yelled. "Remember what happened the last time you started dancing around the table? You need to sit down right now! Your father does not want to wear any more of our dinner."

I quickly sat back down. "Sorry."

"That dance was impressive. You would make a great Indian, honey."

"But what if I pick the turkey?"

"Stop worrying about it, Freddy. It's not the end of the world. If you pick the turkey, then you'll be a turkey. An adorable, plump, feathery, brown turkey."

"That's easy for you to say," I grumbled under my breath. "You don't have to get up in front of everyone and make a fool of yourself."

CHAPTER 3

And the Turkey
Goes to . . .

The next day at recess everyone was talking about the play.

"I can't wait to get our parts. My mom says that I should be the star of the show," said Chloe, tossing her strawberry-blonde curls and smiling her best movie-star smile.

"Of course she does," Jessie whispered in my ear.

"She says that I am the prettiest and the most talented girl in the whole class."

I started to giggle.

"What's so funny, Freddy?" asked Chloe. "Why are you laughing?"

"I'll tell you why he's laughing," Max interrupted. "Because you're a Ding-Dong. A crazy Ding-Dong."

"I am not," Chloe said, stamping her foot. "You take that back right now, Max Sellars, or I'm going to tell Mrs. Wushy."

Max stamped his foot and imitated Chloe. "I'm going to tell Mrs. Wushy," he whined.

We all started giggling.

"Ooohh, stop that!"

"Ooohh, stop that!"

"Stop copying me!"

"Stop copying me!"

"Oh, you make me so mad I'm going to . . ."

I couldn't wait to hear this. What could she possibly do to the biggest bully in the whole first grade?

"What are you going to do?" Max snickered. "Punch me?"

Chloe's face got redder and redder. It was almost the color of her hair. I thought steam was going to come out of her ears. In a huff, she turned and ran toward our teacher, calling, "Mrs. Wushy, Mrs. Wushy . . ."

"That girl is something else," said Robbie.

"Besides," said Jessie, "I don't know what she was talking about. There is no star in this show, and Mrs. Wushy is not giving us our parts. We are picking them out of a hat."

"Did you have to remind me?" I groaned.

"What's your problem?"

"My problem is I don't want to be the turkey."

"The turkey?" said Robbie. "What are you talking about?"

"Suzie did this play when she was in first grade, and last night she told me that someone in the class has to be the turkey."

"Ha, ha, ha!" Max laughed hysterically. "Freddy is a turkey! Freddy is a turkey!"

"Hey, I wouldn't be laughing like that if I were you," said Jessie. "What if you have to be the turkey?"

"Yeah," I said, "that would be the perfect part for you because you're already a big turkey! Ha, ha, ha!"

Max walked over to me and got right in my face. I could feel his hot breath on my cheek. "What did you say, Shark Freak?"

I could feel my heart pounding in my chest. Did I just call Max Sellars a turkey? What was I thinking? He could crush me with one hand. "I said . . . uhhh . . . I said . . ."

Jessie stepped in between Max and me and poked her finger into Max's chest. "He said you were a turkey."

Wow! Jessie was so brave. She always stood up to Max. He never pushed her around. Maybe someday I would be as brave as she was, but today was not the day. I took a few steps backwards.

"That was a close one," said Robbie.

"I know."

"What were you thinking, calling Max Sellars a turkey?"

"I don't know," I whispered.

Just then the bell rang, signaling the end of recess, and we all lined up to go inside.

"Max," said Mrs. Wushy, "were you copying Chloe?"

"Well . . . I . . . uhhh . . ."

"Yes he did, Mrs. Wushy. Yes he did!" Chloe whined.

"Chloe, I am talking to Max right now. You need to be quiet."

"Hmphh," said Chloe, putting her hands on her hips.

"Now, Max, it's a simple question. Did you copy Chloe? Yes or no?"

"Yes," he said quietly.

"What was that? I didn't hear you."

"Yes."

"I have told you many times not to tease the other children. You will have a time-out, and when we go inside and pick our parts for the play, you will pick last."

"But . . . that's not fair," Max protested.

"Oh, it's very fair," said Mrs. Wushy, "and if you want to complain, then maybe you don't have to pick a part at all."

Max stopped arguing and dragged himself inside. Even he knew he'd better be quiet if he wanted to be in the play.

We all sat down on the rug, except for Max, who had to sit in the time-out chair.

"Okay, boys and girls. I know you have been waiting all day to pick your parts for the play, and now it's time."

Jessie squeezed my hand. "Good luck."

I squeezed back. "Good luck to you, too. I hope you get the part you want."

"Here's how it's going to work," continued Mrs. Wushy. "I have written the parts down on little pieces of paper and put them in this hat. When I come around, you will pick one—and only one—piece of paper out of the hat. The papers are folded, and I want you to keep them that way until everyone has had a chance to pick. When everyone has a piece of paper in his or her hand, then I will say, 'One, two, three, look.' Then you may all look at your pieces of paper. Understand?"

We all nodded our heads.

"Any questions?"

"May I pick first, Mrs. Wushy?" asked Chloe.

"No. I am going to go down the rows. Jon will pick first."

As Mrs. Wushy got closer and closer to me,

my heart was beating so fast I thought it was going to pop out of my chest. "OK, Freddy, it's your turn to pick."

"Come on, Indian," I whispered to myself. I felt all around the hat and picked out a slip of paper that I hoped would be lucky.

As Mrs. Wushy continued walking around to all the kids, I squeezed the paper tightly in my hand and rubbed my lucky shark's tooth for good luck.

"And last but not least," said Mrs. Wushy, "Max gets to pick."

"It's not really picking when there's only one left," he grumped.

"As I said before," Mrs. Wushy continued, "you don't have to have a part at all."

"It's the dumb old turkey. I just know it," said Max as he pulled the last piece of paper out of the hat.

"Did I skip anyone?" asked Mrs. Wushy.

We all shook our heads.

"OK then. The big moment has arrived. After I count to three, I will say, 'look,' and then you can all open your papers. Ready? One, two, three, look."

I closed my eyes and slowly unfolded the paper. When I opened my eyes, I thought I was going to throw up. There it was in big letters:

T-U-R-K-E-Y.

CHAPTER 4

Gobble, Gobble

I closed the piece of paper. "I must be seeing things," I thought. "It can't possibly say 'turkey.' There's no way." I slowly opened the paper again, and sure enough, there it was: T-U-R-K-E-Y. No matter how many times I opened and closed the paper, it still said "turkey." No matter how long I stared at it, it still said "turkey."

"My life is over," I groaned.

"What's the matter?" asked Robbie.

"I got it."

"Got what?"

"It."

"What's 'it'?"

"Are you really going to make me say it? 'Turkey'! I got the turkey!"

I must have said it a little too loud because just then everyone in the class turned and looked at me.

Max started laughing, and pointed his finger at me. "Freddy is a turkey! Freddy is a turkey!"

"You see?" I said to Robbie. "My life really is over."

"Now, Max," said Mrs. Wushy, "stop that this minute, or I will send you to Mr. Pendergast's office. I have had just about enough of you today. Besides," continued Mrs. Wushy, "Freddy is very lucky to be the turkey."

"Oh yeah. Really lucky," I muttered to myself.

"The turkey is the symbol of Thanksgiving. It is a very important part of the play."

"That's OK, Mrs. Wushy. I don't have to

have such a big part. Maybe I should trade with someone else." Who was I kidding? No one was going to want to trade for the part of a turkey!

"Remember what I said yesterday, Freddy?"

Chloe piped up, "You get what you get, and you don't get upset."

That's easy for her to say. She didn't pick the turkey!

"We will begin practicing tomorrow, boys and girls, but you can start thinking about your costumes tonight. Have fun and be creative."

The bus ride home was miserable. All the kids were so excited about their parts in the play. Everyone except me.

"I can't believe I got the part of the Indian princess," said Jessie. "That was the one I wanted. She was such a brave girl."

"Just like you," said Robbie.

"Thanks, Robbie. My *abuela* is really good at sewing. She can make me a beautiful dress just like the one the princess wore with all those beads on it. She learned how to make designs with beads when she was a little girl growing up in Mexico."

"I'm going to wear a beautiful dress for my Pilgrim costume, too," said Chloe. "I have the cutest pink dress with red roses on it. My nana brought it all the way from France, and she even bought me shoes to match."

"For your information," said Robbie, "the Pilgrims mostly wore black and white, and their clothes were really plain. They didn't wear anything that had designs on it."

"Well, that's not very fashionable," Chloe said. "Black-and-white clothes are so boring. How can I look like a star in such a plain outfit?"

"Hey, fancy-pants!" yelled Max. "When are you going to get it through your fat head that you are not the star?"

"I am, too. My mother even said so!"

"Well, I've got news for you. Your mother's wrong."

"Oh no she's not!"

"Oh yes she is!"

"Oh no she's not!"

"Oh yes she is!"

I was in such a bad mood that I couldn't listen to them argue any more. I was getting a headache. "Be quiet!" I shouted.

Everyone on the bus stopped talking. It was silent. You could have heard a pin drop.

Then Max slowly turned his head my direction.

"Uh-oh. Here it comes," I thought to myself. I slowly sank down into my seat.

"Well, well, well. Look who's talking. It's the turkey. I didn't even know turkeys could talk."

"Leave him alone," said Jessie. "He's sort of upset right now."

Max leaned over the seat and put his mouth right next to my ear. "Gobble, gobble. Gobble, gobble."

I tried to ignore him, but he wouldn't stop. "Gobble, gobble. Gobble, gobble."

I pulled the hood of my jacket over my head and covered my ears with my hands. This just made Max gobble louder. "GOBBLE, GOBBLE. GOBBLE, GOBBLE!"

Then he started singing a song we had learned in school that day: "'The turkey is a funny bird. His head goes wobble, wobble. The only word that he can say is: gobble, gobble, gobble.'"

Now the other kids on the bus all started laughing.

"Leave him alone!" yelled Jessie.

Max stopped gobbling and looked at her. "Says who?"

"Says me."

"Really? You can't make me."

"Oh yes I can," Jessie said, staring Max right in the eyes.

I peeked out from underneath my hood. Wow! Jessie was even braver than I thought.

"What are you going to do? You're just a girl," Max said, laughing.

"I take karate, so you don't want to mess with me."

The other kids on the bus started chanting, "Jessie, Jessie."

Max stared at her for a minute and said, "We'll finish this later." Then he sat back down in his seat. Secretly I think he was afraid of Jessie, but he would never admit it.

"Thanks, Jessie. That was awesome!"

"No problem. That's what friends are for," she said, patting me on the shoulder. "Max is really just a big baby."

I laughed.

"You see, Freddy? Everything's going to be fine."

I let out a big sigh. I wished I could believe her, but right now I just wanted to crawl into a hole and never come out.

CHAPTER 5

The Secret Plan

As soon as I got home from school, I ran straight to my room and slammed the door.

"Freddy, is that you?" my mom called from downstairs.

I didn't answer. I didn't feel like talking to anyone . . . ever again!

I could hear my mom's footsteps on the stairs. Why couldn't she leave me alone? I got into bed and pulled the covers over my head.

She knocked on the door. "Freddy, honey, are you in there?"

No answer.

"Freddy, are you all right?"

No answer.

"Freddy? Freddy?" She started to turn the door handle.

"LEAVE ME ALONE!" I shouted.

"What's wrong, sweetie?"

"NOTHING! NOW GO AWAY!"

I'm not sure what part of "go away" she didn't understand, but the next thing I knew she opened the door and walked in.

"I SAID, GO AWAY!"

She came over to the bed and sat down.

"Are you feeling all right, honey?" she asked, trying to pull the covers off my head. "Let me feel your forehead to see if you have a temperature."

I held on to the covers tightly. "NO! I DON'T HAVE A TEMPERATURE!"

"Well, something must be wrong. You always come home and go straight to the kitchen for a snack."

"I'M NOT HUNGRY!"

"If you're not hungry, then I definitely know something's not right—because you always want to eat!"

Just when I thought she was never going to leave the room, Suzie came home from school. "Oh, that sounds like Suzie. I'll go check on her, and then I'll be right back."

"Take your time," I said from underneath the covers.

After I heard her footsteps disappear down the hall, I sat up in bed and hit my forehead with the palm of my hand. "Think, think, think." I had to come up with a plan. There was no way I was going to get up in front of everyone in a dumb turkey costume. And Max would call me turkey and gobble, gobble in my ear for the rest of my life.

Just then a great idea popped into my head. Maybe I could run away until after Thanksgiving. I could disappear until after the show was over,

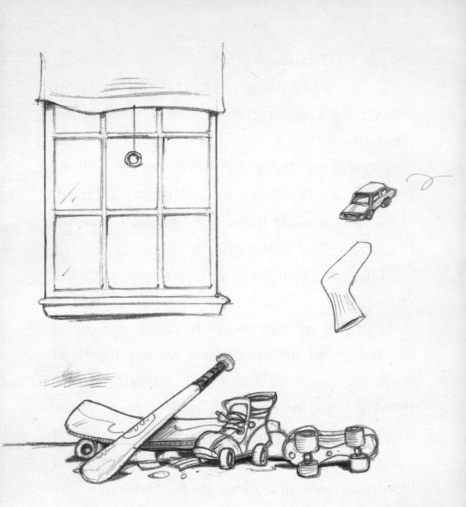

and then I'd come back. Why didn't I think of this before?

I ran to my closet to look for my suitcase on wheels, my favorite one with the big hammer-head shark on it. My closet was such a mess I

couldn't find it at first. I pulled out my base-
ball bat, my roller skates, and my skateboard.
I finally found the suitcase hidden behind the
big blow-up shark I won at the carnival last
month.

I dragged it out of the closet, set it down on my bed, and stared at it for a long time. What do you need to pack if you are going to run away? I had never run away before, so I really had no idea. I started with the easy stuff: underwear, a few pairs of pants, some shirts, my favorite shark pajamas. So far so good. Of course I would have to take the Dream Police: Chompers, Eddie, and Bananas. I couldn't sleep without my special stuffed animals, and they would protect me from anything bad that might happen. I looked around the room. What else? What else?

Oh! A picture of the family. I would have to take one with me so I could remember what they looked like. I didn't have a picture in my room, so I would have to sneak out and borrow one from the dresser in my parents' room. My mom had all kinds of family pictures on her dresser, so she would never notice if one of them was missing.

I slowly opened my bedroom door and peeked out to make sure the coast was clear. My mom and Suzie were still downstairs. I tiptoed to my parents' room and grabbed a picture of the whole family at the beach last summer. I hid it under my shirt and quickly tiptoed back to my room.

I stuck it in the suitcase under my pajamas and sat back down on my bed to think. As I was sitting there deciding what else to pack, I heard footsteps on the stairs. Oh great! My mom was coming back. I couldn't let her see the suitcase, so I quickly shoved it under the bed and jumped back under the covers. I did it just in time, too, because she didn't even knock. She just barged right in.

"Freddy, are you still hiding under there?"

Then came Suzie, two steps behind. "What's he doing?"

"GO AWAY! BOTH OF YOU!"

"Someone's in a bad mood," said Suzie.

"WHO INVITED YOU IN HERE, ANYWAY?"

"Someone's got a case of the grumpies," Suzie said and laughed.

"LEAVE ME ALONE!"

As my mom came closer to me, she tripped on the handle of my suitcase. It was sticking out slightly from underneath the bed. My mom fell on top of me.

"OOOWWWW!" I shrieked.

"I'm so sorry, Freddy. It was an accident. I just tripped on something on your floor. I think it was this thing here."

Before I could stop her, she reached down and pulled out the suitcase. "A suitcase? Why is your suitcase under your bed? I asked you to keep it in your closet."

My mom is a neat freak, so everything always has to be put back in the right place. Under the bed was not the right place for a suitcase. "I'm going to put it back in the closet."

When she lifted the suitcase to put it back,

it must have felt heavy, so she stopped and started to unzip it. "What's in here, Freddy? Did you forget to unpack it from our last . . ."

"Wait!" I yelled. I jumped off the bed and sailed through the air, trying to grab the suitcase before she could open it all the way. Instead, I missed and landed with a *thud* on the floor.

"Oh my goodness! Freddy, are you all right?"

I stared up at her from the floor. "Yeah," I said weakly. "I think so."

"What has gotten into you? You are acting so strangely."

"And why is your suitcase packed?" Suzie interrupted. "Are you planning on going somewhere?"

Great! Just great! While I was lying on the floor, my busybody sister had opened my suit-case all the way, and now she and my mom could see everything.

"Freddy, enough of these games. Either you tell me what's going on here, or you are in big trouble, mister!"

CHAPTER 6

Turkey Trouble

"I . . . was . . . going . . . to . . . run . . . away . . ."
I said, beginning to sob.

"Run away?" said my mom.

"Run away?" echoed Suzie.

"Why on earth would you want to run away,
honey?"

"Because . . . I'm . . . a . . . tu-tu-turkey!" I
wailed.

"A turkey? What are you talking about?"

"Oh, I think I know what he's talking about,"
said Suzie.

"Well, would you please fill me in? Because

right now your brother is not making any sense."

"Freddy, did you pick your parts for the play today?"

I nodded my head.

"Did you pick the turkey?" asked Suzie.

"Y-y-yes!" I wailed. "My life is over! I never want to show my face at school again!" I wiped my runny nose on my sleeve.

"Oh, Freddy, is that what this is all about?" asked my mom, giving me a hug and handing me a Kleenex. "Would you use this, please, instead of your sleeve?"

I grabbed the Kleenex from her and blew my nose hard.

"Careful," said Suzie, chuckling. "You wouldn't want to blow your brains out, or at least the few brains you have."

"Suzie," said my mom, "this is not a time for jokes. You need to apologize to your brother."

"Sorry, Freddy. I was just kidding. I was trying to make you feel better. Being the turkey really isn't that bad."

"But you said so yourself. You said no one in your class wanted to be the turkey. You said it was a bad part."

"It is not a bad part," said my mom.

"Yes it is. It's the worst part in the whole play, and that's why I decided to run away and not come back until after the play is over. Don't worry, though. I'll be back in time for Thanksgiving dinner with Papa and Grammy. I wouldn't miss that."

My mom stared at me for a minute and then said, "I think I know exactly what you need."

"What?"

"Don't go anywhere. I'll be right back." She left the room.

"Run away?" said Suzie. "I can't believe you

were going to run away. I know you can be a real pain sometimes, but I would be really sad if you ran away."

"Really?"

"Yeah, really. Where were you going to go?"

"I'm not sure. I hadn't decided yet."

"You were going to run away, but you didn't even know where you were going to go?"

"Yeah," I said, laughing. "Sounds kind of crazy, huh?"

"Really crazy! Hey, what else did you have in this little suitcase of yours?" Suzie asked, feeling around inside. "Any snacks?"

"Nah. You know Mom doesn't like us to bring any food into our rooms."

"What's this?" Suzie said, pulling out the family picture.

Oh no! I had forgotten it was in there.

"Isn't this the picture from Mom's dresser?"

I didn't answer. I hoped she would put it down and look through the rest of the stuff.

"Freddy, isn't this the picture from Mom's dresser?" she asked again. "Did you steal it?"

I could see she wasn't going to let this one go. "I didn't exactly steal it. I just borrowed it for my trip. I was planning on bringing it back home."

"Mom is going to be sooooo mad when she finds out you took this. It's one of her favorite pictures."

"She doesn't have to know. I can just put it back before she notices."

"But I know," Suzie said, smiling.

"You don't have to tell her."

"What's it worth to you?"

"Ummm . . . I don't know."

"Well, I do," said Suzie. "Your new golden-dollar coin you got from the Tooth Fairy."

"But . . . but . . . but I just got that."

"Do we have a deal or not?" Suzie asked, holding up her pinkie for a pinkie swear.

I could hear my mom coming back down the hall. Suzie was right. We were never supposed to take our mom's things without permission. "Deal," I said as we locked pinkies.

"Freddy," my mom said, as she walked into the room carrying the phone. "Someone wants to talk to you."

CHAPTER 7

Let's Talk Turkey

"Who is it?" I asked.

My mom handed me the phone.

"Why don't you answer it and find out?"

"Hello?"

"Hello, Freddy. Is that you?"

I'd recognize that voice anywhere. It was Papa Dave. "Yeah, Papa, it's me."

"Your mom tells me you are planning on running away."

"Well, I was."

"But why? Why would you want to run away?"

"Because I'm a turkey."

"A what?"

"A turkey."

"Says who?"

"Says my teacher, Mrs. Wushy."

"Your teacher called you a turkey?"

"Well, not exactly."

"Freddy, you'd better start from the beginning, because I don't understand what's going on."

"OK, Papa. Here's the story. My class is doing a play for Thanksgiving."

"That sounds like fun."

"I thought so, too, until we had to pick our parts out of a hat."

"What did you pick?"

"The turkey! The worst part in the whole play! Now everybody won't stop teasing me, and Max the bully keeps gobbling in my face. That's why I decided to run away."

"Freddy, let me tell you something. Running away never solved anyone's problems."

"It didn't?"

"No, sir. You have to face your problems head-on. Not run away from them."

"That's easy for you to say, Papa Dave. You don't have to be laughed at every day at school, and you don't have to get up in front of all the parents and make a fool of yourself."

"I would love to be the turkey."

"You would? Why?"

"Because it's the best part."

"No, it's not, Papa. You're wrong."

"Listen, Freddy, if you are a Pilgrim or an Indian, then you are just like all the other kids in the play."

"Yeah, that would be great. I'd love to be a Pilgrim or an Indian."

"No, you wouldn't. If you're just like everybody else, then no one will remember you. But if you're different, then everyone will remember you for a very long time."

"Huh?"

"What I'm trying to say is that it's good to be different."

"But what about Max?"

"Are you really going to let a little gobbling get to you like that? You show him that you are proud to be a turkey. If he gobbles at you, then just gobble right back in his face, loud and proud."

"Ha, ha, ha! That's funny, Papa. I don't think he'll know what to do."

"No, he won't. You just wobble your head, flap your wings, and gobble, gobble, gobble—until he turns and runs the other way. Trust me . . . he will."

I giggled. "I can't wait to do that tomorrow, Papa."

"Promise you'll call me and tell me what Max does."

"I promise."

"And promise me one more thing."

"What?"

"That you won't run away from home."

"I promise."

"You know I love you very much. I want to see your smiling face when I come for Thanksgiving, and I want to see you strut your stuff onstage. You know Grammy and I will be there in time to see your show."

"You will?"

"Yep. And I want to tell everyone, 'See that big, fat turkey up there on that stage? He's my grandson. He's the symbol of Thanksgiving. He's the star of the show!'"

"Thanks, Papa. You always make me feel better. I can't wait to see you and Grammy."

"Make me proud, Freddy. Be the best turkey Lincoln Elementary has ever seen!"

CHAPTER 8

Loud and Proud

After the little talk with Papa Dave, I had no problem with being the turkey. In fact, I was excited to play the part.

The day of the show finally arrived. I was up even before my alarm went off. I wanted to make sure I had all the parts of my costume ready to take to school. My mom had worked really hard making me the best turkey costume ever, and I didn't want to forget a piece of it.

I looked in the bag. Brown pants and shirt. Check. Turkey feet. Check. Socks. Check. Feather suit. Check. Hood with beak. Ch—oh no! Where was the hood? That was the best part of the costume.

I looked under my bed. Not there. I looked in my closet. Not there. I looked behind my bookcase. Not there.

I ran to look in the bathroom. Maybe I left it in there last night when I was trying on my costume in front of the mirror. Of course when I got to the bathroom, it was locked. Princess Suzie was making herself look beautiful for school.

I pounded on the door. "Open up, Suzie. It's an emergency!"

"You'll have to wait your turn, Shark Breath. I'm busy right now."

"But I need to get in—right away!"

"Too bad."

I pounded on the door even harder. "Let me in! Let me in!"

"Freddy, what is the problem?" asked my mom. "I heard you all the way downstairs in the kitchen."

"I can't find my hood, Mom. And that's the best part of my costume! I won't look like a turkey without it."

"Calm down. Why don't you look in your room?"

"I already did. It's not there. That's why I want to check the bathroom, but Stinky Suzie won't let me in."

"Suzie," my mom said, knocking gently on the door. "Please open the door. Your brother needs to look for something in there."

"Sure thing, Mom," Suzie said, opening the door and smiling sweetly. "I don't know what Freddy was yelling about."

When my mom wasn't looking, I stuck my tongue out at her and whispered, "Brat."

"Oh look, Freddy. Here it is," said my mom, lifting the hood out of the dirty-clothes hamper. "I wonder how it got in there?"

"Yeah, I wonder," I said, staring at Suzie. "Thanks for finding it, Mom. You're the best."

"No problem, honey. Now go put it in the bag with the rest of the costume and come downstairs for breakfast. A turkey has to eat a good breakfast, you know—to stay nice and fat."

In true turkey fashion, I gobbled down my breakfast. Then I headed off to school. Our classroom was buzzing with excitement.

"Today is the big day, boys and girls. All of your families are coming to see the Thanksgiving show. I know they are going to be so proud of you! Right now you all need to put on your costumes."

"I'm so excited about my dress," said Jessie. "My *abuela* worked really hard sewing it. She made this beaded necklace. It's so beautiful."

"I love my costume, too," I said. "My mom spent hours sewing it. That dress is really pretty," I said to Jessie. "You look just like an Indian princess."

"Thanks!"

"What about me, Freddy?" Chloe interrupted,

stepping right in front of Jessie. "Don't I look beautiful?"

I just stared at her.

"Well, what do you guys think?" she asked, twirling around in her black-and-white Pilgrim dress.

"He thinks you're a pain," Max butted in. "Freddy wasn't talking to you. He was talking to Jessie."

"You don't have to be so mean, Max Sellars," Chloe whined, sticking out her lower lip.

"And you don't have to be so annoying."

I carefully took my costume out of the bag. I didn't want any of the feathers to break off. Just as I started to put it on, I heard it. The giggling was quiet at first, but then it got louder and louder. I turned around and saw all of the kids in the class laughing at me. Not just Max, but everyone!

My cheeks got hot, and my face turned as red as a tomato. I dropped the costume and ran out of the room.

"Freddy, wait!" Mrs. Wushy called as she ran after me.

I didn't want to wait. I just wanted to keep running and never go back to that classroom again. I wanted to hide. But where? I stopped for a second and hit my forehead with the palm of my hand. "Think, think, think."

When I looked up, I saw the janitor coming out of a supply closet. As soon as he turned his back and headed down the hall, I ran inside and hid next to the big vacuum cleaner. I was scared because it was really dark in there, but sitting in the dark was still better than having all the kids in my class laugh at me. I sat there for a while, frozen like a statue, trying not to make a sound.

I could hear footsteps coming closer. I held my breath. "Freddy! Freddy!" Mrs. Wushy called. "Where are you?"

Just then I heard another voice. It was Mr. Pendergast, the principal.

"Is something wrong, Mrs. Wushy?"

"Yes, Mr. Pendergast. I'm looking for Freddy Thresher. He ran away."

"Ran away? What do you mean?"

"Well, the other children in the class were laughing at him about his costume for the Thanksgiving show, and he got really upset and ran out of the room. I can't find him anywhere!"

"That's terrible. Where do you think he went?"

"I have no idea, and I'm getting worried."

"Maybe we'd better call the police," Mr. Pendergast said.

The police! I didn't want to be the turkey, but I didn't want to go to jail, either!

I jumped up and threw open the door. "I don't want to go to jail!" I howled. Then I burst into tears. "I'm sorry!"

"Freddy. Thank goodness you're all right," Mrs. Wushy said, giving me a hug. "Don't worry. You're not going to jail."

"But I heard you say you were going to call the police!"

"We just thought the police could help us find you," said Mr. Pendergast. "They weren't going to take you to jail," he said with a smile.

"Oh, Freddy," said Mrs. Wushy, "I'm so sorry the kids laughed at you like that. I think your costume is beautiful."

"No it's not," I cried. "It's stupid, and everyone is going to laugh at me. I'm not going to be in the play!"

"But you have to be. The turkey is the star of the show. It's the symbol of Thanksgiving."

"Then someone else can be the turkey, because I am not going to do it."

"Freddy," said Mr. Pendergast, "why don't you come to my office. I want to tell you a little story."

"Am I in trouble?"

"No, of course not. I just want to talk to you for a minute."

He took my hand and led me into his office.

I'm sure Max could describe every detail, but I'd never been in there before.

"Take a seat."

I sat down in a big, cushy chair across from Mr. Pendergast's desk. I thought the chair was going to swallow me up!

"Freddy, do you know what part I had in my first-grade play?"

I shook my head.

"A piece of trash."

I tried not to laugh, but I couldn't help it. "A piece of trash?" I asked and giggled.

"Yep. A piece of trash. My class was doing a play about recycling, and I had to be a piece of trash. I was so embarrassed, and everybody teased me for weeks."

"So what did you do?"

"Well, at first I cried about it like you did, and I told my mom that I was never going to school again."

"Did she let you stay home?"

"Of course not. And since I had no choice, I decided to be the best piece of trash anybody ever saw. I decided to be a dancing piece of trash."

"A dancing piece of trash! That sounds hilarious."

"Oh, it was! And everybody loved it. In fact, my teacher said I stole the show!"

"Really?"

"Really. So how about it? Want to be the dancing turkey?"

I jumped up out of my seat and started dancing around Mr. Pendergast's office. "Gobble, gobble. Gobble, gobble."

Mr. Pendergast laughed, and then he started gobbling and dancing around his office, too! I never knew that he could be so funny.

"All right, Freddy. You'd better hurry, or you'll miss the show!"

I ran back to my classroom and got there just as everyone was lining up to go to the auditorium.

Jessie smiled and said, "Hurry, Freddy. It's almost time for the show. We need you!"

Mrs. Wushy helped me into my costume.

Jessie squeezed my hand. "Good luck, Freddy," she whispered. "You look great!"

I squeezed her hand back. "Good luck to you, too."

When we got to the auditorium, the parents and grandparents were already there.

"Come on, everyone," called Mrs. Wushy. "Get backstage. It's almost time to start the show."

As I started to head backstage, Papa Dave walked over to me and whispered, "Go get 'em, Tiger. Remember: loud and proud. Gobble, gobble!" Then he gave me a quick hug and went to his seat.

As the curtains opened, I looked out into the audience and saw Mr. Pendergast standing in the back of the auditorium. He flapped his arms and did a silent gobble. I smiled. Then I strutted out on stage, flapped my wings, and did my loudest and proudest GOBBLE, GOBBLE, GOBBLE!

The audience laughed, Papa Dave, Grammy, and Mr. Pendergast cheered, and I began the show: "Welcome to our class play about the story of Thanksgiving . . ."

DEAR READER,

I love Thanksgiving because I love the good food, getting together with my family, and sharing memories.

Once when I was little, I wanted to help my mom cook the Thanksgiving dinner. She had just started making mashed potatoes when the phone rang, so she asked me to turn on the mixer and mash them up. I didn't realize that you had to lock the mixer in place before you turned it on, so I just hit the start switch and mashed potatoes started flying everywhere! There was potato goo on the kitchen walls, on the floor, all over my face, and dripping off my hair. What a mess! My mom didn't think it was very funny at the time, but now we look back on it and laugh.

I'm sure you have a special Thanksgiving memory, and you're thankful for many things.

I hope you have as much fun reading *Thanksgiving Turkey Trouble* as I had writing it.

HAPPY READING!

Freddy's Fun Pages

FREDDY'S SHARK JOURNAL

WHAT DO SHARKS FEAST ON?

Sharks eat almost any creature found in the sea, from the smallest plankton to the largest seals.

Some sharks even eat other sharks!

Great white sharks are probably the hungriest sharks. They are hunting and eating most of the time.

Most sharks do not eat every day. Most eat one big meal every two to three days.

If there is not a lot of food, sharks can even go for weeks without eating.

PINECONE TURKEY

Being a turkey isn't so bad! Try a turkey activity for your next Thanksgiving celebration.

YOU WILL NEED:

a pinecone

glue

yellow, red, and orange felt

two googly eyes

one brown pom-pom

pipe cleaners of various colors

1. Use the felt to cut out a yellow beak, a red wattle, and two orange feet.

2. Glue the beak, wattle, and two wiggly eyes onto the brown pom-pom.

3. Glue the pom-pom head to the pointed end of the pinecone.

4. For the turkey's tail, individually wrap three or four pipe cleaners around the back of the pinecone and twist the pipe cleaners together a few times on the top of the pinecone to secure them.

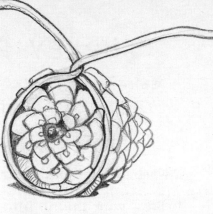

5. Loop the end of each pipe cleaner to shape the tail feathers.

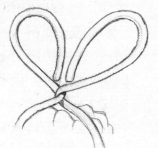

6. Glue the felt feet on to the bottom of the pinecone.

TURKEY PLACECARD

Make placecards for each person who will be at your Thanksgiving table.

YOU WILL NEED:

a washable ink pad, markers, and small paper cards

1. Press your thumb into the ink pad and then press it sideways on the paper to make the turkey's body.

2. Press your fingertips into the inkpad and then press them on the paper, fanning around the thumbprint to make the turkey's tail feathers. Add another fingerprint to make the head.

3. Use markers to draw a beak, wattle, eyes, and feet.

4. Write one of your guests' names on each card.

HARVEST NECKLACE

Jessie's abuela made her a beaded necklace.
You can make your own out of snacks.

YOU WILL NEED:

a large needle

about 36 inches of
  string, fishing line,
  or heavy-duty thread

popcorn

raisins, cranberries, or
  other small dried fruit

round cereal bits

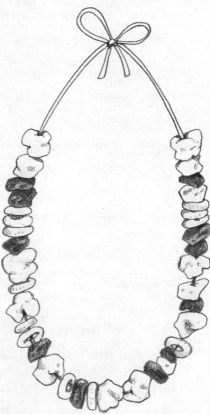

1. Thread the needle
and string the popcorn
and other items in any
order you like. Freddy
likes to mix them up.

2. Leave enough string
for tying off the ends.

3. After you're finished
wearing your necklace you can
hang it outside on a branch to share with the birds.

Have you read all about Freddy?

Don't miss any
of Freddy's
funny adventures!